Say 'Hello'

to Peter Ian Green

– 'PIG' for short.

There are six PIG books so far. It's best to
read them in this order:

1. **Pig** and the **Talking Poo**
2. **Pig** and the **Fancy Pants**
3. **Pig** and the **Long Fart**
4. **Pig** plays **Cupid**
5. **Pig** gets the **Black Death** (nearly)
6. **Pig** **Saves** the **Day**

PIG and the Fancy Pants
by Barbara Catchpole
Illustrated by metaphrog

Published by Ransom Publishing Ltd.
Unit 7, Brocklands Farm, West Meon, Hampshire
GU32 1JN, UK
www.ransom.co.uk

ISBN   978 184167 523 7
First published in 2012
Reprinted 2013, 2014, 2015 (twice)

PIG

and the Fancy

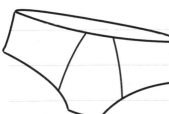

Pants

Barbara Catchpole

Illustrated by metaphrog

Rans♦m

Me again

Hi, here I am again. It's me, Pig!

I really want to tell you about this thing that happened to me the other day. This story is about how I had no pants for school. (I mean underpants: tighty whities - even though they're never white. Even the white ones.)

The school counsellor decided that I should go on this surfing holiday because I had no pants. Really! I don't know why! You know adults - they're so random.

Surfing is where you go to the seaside and balance on a board on a big wave. Like the beginning of 'You Only Live Twice' or 'Hawaii Five-O'.

I bet I'm just like James Bond - but ginger, of course.

My mum said I was

'a jammy little tike'

and I

 'deserved a good hiding, let alone a holiday.'

But then she said:

 'Someone in this house might as well have a holiday,'

and

 'At least it's free,'

and

 'If they knew what he's like, they wouldn't take him nowhere without handcuffs and a taser,'

and

    'At least WE'LL get some peace and quiet,'

and

    'We should move house before he gets
    back.'

Before I get her in all sorts of trouble, she only says 'a good hiding' because it's something HER mum said to her.

My mum can think of some pretty cruel punishments though. She once made me clean the kitchen floor with an old toothbrush.

I'm busting to tell you the Great Story of the Frilly Pants and how I was awarded a surfing holiday for wearing frilly pants. But first I'll tell you about my dead-boring family, so you know what's going on.

Mum

Mum is doing pottery evening classes.

'Not just a pretty face, am I? I need to get out and meet people.'

I hope she's meeting loads of nice people because she's rubbish at pottery.

Gran said she hoped Mum met a rich bloke and he fell in love with her. Then he bought us all a big house on the posh estate and then she got to go to bingo in a taxi every day.

I said perhaps she would meet Johnny Depp, but Gran didn't think he would do pottery at Coalpits High School evening classes. He probably does pottery in Hollywood.

Johnny Depp →

HOLLYWOOD

← pottery

I think Mum may be hoping too, because we don't seem to have much money now Dad has left. She has to buy those nasty, manky baked beans to save money, but they don't taste the same and the sauce is like water.

Anyway I hope she gets better at pots, because at the moment she just brings home ugly lumps of clay.

You can't call them pots because they fall over and they don't hold water (for long). One fell on Gran's foot and nearly broke it. She hopped on one foot for ages and said some very bad words. (She's allowed to say bad words because she's old. Gran knows a LOT of bad words!)

The pots are usually the colour of baby poo and they sit on the window ledge. I wouldn't have them on MY window ledge if you paid me.

Mum would go:

'Here, Pig, have five pounds to look after
this pot.'

I would go:

'No way, Mum, that is one ugly pot. I don't
want to mess up my window ledge.'

I do use one to wedge my door shut though. You
know, when I'm doing stuff.

Gran

Gran was poorly. I think she had the flu. She
kept saying

'I'm not long for this world!'

and Mum kept saying

'You'll live 'til you're a hundred, you!'

Gran is 72 and a half now. When I leave school, I'm going to be a film star like Johnny Depp (only ginger). So I'll have to come back from being a film star in Hollywood on my private plane to go to Gran's funeral.

I told her that and she said:

'Don't put yourself out just for me. I don't want to stop you starring in films and marrying blonde models for a day just to go to my funeral.'

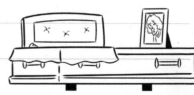

Suki

I never thought about girls' underwear before – but now I know, I can't talk to Suki without going red. And she's my SISTER!

To be honest, at the moment I go red when I talk to any girl. I hope it wears off soon. It's just that now I know what they are wearing under their clothes.

Underwear

Baby

Still smelly. Still doesn't sleep. He crawls a bit now though.

Last week Mum said he had dire rear (I'm sure that's what she said – it sounded like that anyway). His nappy leaked and it went everywhere. It turned the kitchen floor into a skating rink.

Hamster

We thought Harry was going to die because I

thought it might like a toffee – so I fed it one.
The toffee got stuck in its pouch and Mum had
to get it out with a lolly stick.

Then it bit her and she shouted at me and said
she was going to sell me on eBay. (Again!) Just
something she says – I hope.

That's it really. The only other thing that's
happened is Pants. Oh yeah, I was busting to
tell you about it. It happened like this ...

Monday, oh eight hundred hours

Mum says she yelled upstairs three times, but I was having this brilliant dream about how I was in the England football team and everyone said it was rubbish because I was only twelve.

I was in goal because I get puffed if I have to run without my inhaler.

We were playing Brazil and it was three – three with two minutes to play, when suddenly the other team all ran towards my goal. Lionel Messi fell over and George Best tripped over him (yes I know, but it WAS a dream). Lucky England had me!

The Brazil players all had a football each and they all took a shot at goal, about ten shots, and I saved each one.

Then everybody in my team was hugging me and shaking me and shaking me really, really hard. It was Mum! She was shaking me!

'I thought you had got up! For heaven's sakes, Pig. You could sleep for England! Were you having a dream? You were kicking the duvet like anything and you hugged the pillow!

'Look, I've got to go or I'll be late for work. Take the key off the hook by the door so you can get back in. Your clothes are on the chair in the Kitchen. Now get up!

'DON'T GO BACK TO SLEEP!'

They probably heard three doors down. No wonder the neighbours hate us.

I heard the door slam and I got up and went down to the Kitchen. I like getting dressed in the Kitchen because it's warm. My bedroom is like a freezer. A penguin would move out of my room looking for warmth.

Polar bears would stand and shiver.

Eskimos would find my bedroom a bit chilly.

If I take a drink up to bed
with me, I have to break
the ice on it to drink it.

The kitchen is nice and warm though. My uniform
was over the chair, just where Mum had said.

PJs off and there I
was, standing in all
my glory. I have a
great body. Very buff.

(I heard that! How rude! If you're reading my
book, you have to be nice to me. I am not

weedy! I am a very good looking boy: short, but gorgeous.)

Anyway, I go to put on my underpants and there they weren't! No pants! I was pantless! A pant-free zone.

OK, no panic. Think, Pig, think!

I strode over to the washing basket, still in the nuddy – and there were NO PANTS. At least there were no Pig Pants. What to do? I thought of going to school with no pants on, but I knew:

A.   I wouldn't be able to think in class with no pants on

B.   It would hurt my bits

and

C.   With my luck I would split my trousers
and everyone would see my bum.

So then I thought I would put on my mum's
pants. So I did.

They were huge! They didn't touch me anywhere.
She is One Big Panty Woman. I looked like a
small hovercraft. I tried, but I couldn't stuff
the material into my trousers.

OK. What about my sister's
knickers? She has a tiny
bum - not that I look at it
- EVER - but it is tiny. If
she stands sideways, you
can't see her at all. Her
earrings are the biggest
thing about her and Mum
says she can pick up Sky Television on them.

OK. Back to my sister's pants. There were some

of those things that are just a bit of string. Do you have a sister? Well those things are called thongs. The string bit goes up between your bum so that people can't see your pants.

You would think girls would want people to know they have pants on – but no! I have no idea why. Girls are weird.

Finally I found a pair big enough to see. I held them up. They were made of this shiny stuff and were bright pink with green frilly ribbon round the outside. The front had little sparkles and the words:

DRAMA DIVA

in silver stitching with big silver stars. I tried

them on and they felt very strange. There was no support, if you know what I mean. I did a little dance and they seemed to hold up OK though.

(Isn't it cool when books go dot, dot, dot, dot? I do it in English all the time when I can't think how to end a story – and I'm doing it now:)

Anyway, nobody would see my pants. OR SO I THOUGHT ...

Oh eight oh five hours

I forgot my door key, of course! So I could not get back into the house if I needed to ...

Which turned out to be a bit of a problem ......

Trouble is, once you start using the dots, it's difficult to stop ....

Raj and I walked along to school. We both go to Coalpits High School – everyone calls it 'The Pits'.

Me:

'You'll never guess – I'm wearing my sister's pants.'

Raj:

'You'll never guess – we've got PE this
morning.

'And Kevin Hardwick is in our group. And
most of his gang.

'You are dead.

'You are
SOOOOOO dead.

'Dead. Deady, dead,
dead. Dead city.

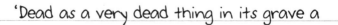

'Dead as a very dead thing in its grave a

29

thousand years after it died.

'Could you walk with somebody else, please?'

Oh nine hundred hours

Here was my plan:

1. Get PE shorts from locker. (Done that. Easy.)

2. Get out of Maths with the dentist card I just happen to keep in my bag. Change into PE shorts – anywhere!

3. Stay in PE shorts under trousers for the

Raj:

'You'll never guess – we've got PE this

morning.

'And Kevin Hardwick is in our group. And

most of his gang.

'You are dead.

'You are

SOOOOOO dead.

'Dead. Deady, dead,

dead. Dead city.

'Dead as a very dead thing in its grave a

thousand years after it died.

'Could you walk with somebody else, please?'

Oh nine hundred hours

Here was my plan:

1. Get PE shorts from locker. (Done that. Easy.)

2. Get out of Maths with the dentist card I just happen to keep in my bag. Change into PE shorts – anywhere!

3. Stay in PE shorts under trousers for the

rest of day. It would be hot in Diva pants,
shorts and trousers – but at least I would
not be the butt (ha ha) of classroom jokes.

Me:

'Please, Sir, I have to
go to the dentist!'

Sir:

'Wrong date on
this card.'

Me:

'I feel sick, Sir!'

Sir:

'I'll open a window.

Stop moaning, Tiffany,

it's not cold.'

Me:

'I'm very upset, Sir. My hamster died.'

Sir:

'They do that. I fed mine a Gummy Bear

once and it died straight away.'

Me:

'I need to go to

the toilet.'

Sir:

    'Me too, Pig. I'm holding on 'til break.'

Me:

    'Sir!'

Sir:

    'No, Pig!'

Me:

    'But ...'

Sir:

    'No!'

Oh ten hundred hours

(I know 'Oh ten hundred hours' is wrong, but it sounds awesome. Like you're doing something REALLY important.)

I made my escape by hiding in the toilets and running down the stairs when Corridor Patrol Bloke went into a classroom. Raj was going to answer the next register for me.

I edged down the stairs like Jack Bauer in pretty pants. There was a huge plant in reception. Perhaps I could hide behind that.

RECEPTION

Yes! I was just edging my way out of my trousers when I felt something wet on my bottom area. The nice West Indian cleaning lady was spraying the plants. I pulled my trousers up quickly, but not before my bottom was good and wet.

'Hello, Pig! What are you doing behind the plant?'

'I'm looking for greenfly, Miss. It's my job.'

'Just in your socks?'

'Er, that's so I can sneak up on them and they don't escape.'

'Do you find many?'

'No.'

'I'm not surprised – the plant's plastic!'

She was another big lady with a big laugh.

I only had forty minutes left and my bottom was now wet with cleaning spray.

Oh ten hundred twenty

I ducked into the hall where there was a big art display on screens. Screens! Just what I needed!

Shoes off and I started to wiggle down my trousers. I just had them down below my bottom when I heard a giggle. The screen was pulled to one side. I just pulled my trousers back up in time. There was a whole class and Mrs Blake looking at me.

'Hello Pig! What are you doing behind the screen?'

'I'm checking the floor for – er – splinters. It's my job.'

'Just in your socks?'

'I feel them with my feet.'

'You are bonkers, Peter Ian Green. Go back to your class!'

I had thirty minutes left.

Oh ten hundred thirty

This is it! I'm in the back of the English stockroom in my underpants. My trousers are around my ankles. I'm about to take my shoes off, when:

'Hallo, Miss.'

'Hallo, Sir.'

'I had a lovely time yesterday evening, Karen.'

'So did I, Lee.'

'How about a little kissy in the stockroom? A little cuddly wuddly kissy wissy for your loverboy?'

It was Miss Hardcastle, my art teacher, and Mr Strange, my PE teacher. A little kissy? A little cuddly? Teachers kissing? I was very nearly sick.

Really I WAS a bit sick, just in my mouth. Luckily I managed to swallow it. (I bet that's happened to you, too. It's gross isn't it? You can taste it for the rest of the day.)

Anyway, I ran for it. Their voices came after me:

'What are you doing in the stockroom, Pig?'

I think: what were THEY doing is a better question.

Great, now Mr Strange (LEE! - yeuch) knows I'm in school. If I skip PE, I'll have detention for a term and Mum will make me clean the street with a toothbrush.

Or I can show my pretty pants to the whole class.

I have ten minutes! Where, oh where, can I get changed?

Oh ten hundred fifty —
the Secret Door

In reception there is a Secret Door. Nobody ever uses it. Nobody knows where it leads.

As I ran through reception, I saw that the Secret Door was open. Really scared now, I quickly slipped inside.

Inside, it was a wonderland: a toilet, but not as we know it.

It smelled, but in a good way. It was a lovely pink colour, even the toilet and the sink. It had a vase of pink flowers on a little table. It had a pink, splodgy painting on the wall. It had a little pink carpet. It had soft bog roll.

I wanted to grow old in that toilet and maybe
die there, sitting on the loo.

I shut the door. I took off my shoes and got
out of my trousers.

I was standing there in my pretty girl's Drama

Diva pants when the headteacher let herself in to her Private Washroom.

For some reason she screamed.

'Waaaaaaaaaaaaaaaaaaaaaaaaaahhhhhhhh
hhhhhhhhhhhhhhhhhhhhhhhhhhhhhhhhhhh
hhhhhhhhhhhhhhhhhhhhhhhhhhhhhhhhhhh
hhhhhhhhhhhhhhhh!'

Oh eleven hundred hours

The headteacher sent me to the school counsellor.

I don't know what he does, so don't ask me. The headteacher said she might have to go and see him herself after the shock. What a fuss! I don't know what was so shocking. I mean, at least I was wearing pants.

Anyway, I didn't know she had a toilet. I didn't even know she WENT to the toilet. I thought she was, like, Superwoman.

Now I want to be clear on this. I was not crying in the school counsellor's office. I don't cry. I am a Bad Influence, I know. I had something in my eye and I had to rub them a bit, that's all. Then, of course, they got a bit watery.

I was not upset or crying at all.

Twenty hundred hours

My sister was out in the garden, burning her Drama Diva pants.

Mum read the school letter about what had

happened. She cried.
Tears ran down her
cheeks from the laughter.

She even snorted and I
think she let out a tiny
fart as well. It's hard
to tell when girls fart – they seem to be able
to control it better than boys. It doesn't smell
so much either.

Anyway, the school counsellor had written this
letter. I have to say the man is mad as cheese.
He kept going on about roll models and how I
didn't have one now Dad had left us.

I don't think Dad'll come back either, because Mum is in a right strop with him!

Anyway, Dad is not a model. He's not even good looking! He doesn't make rolls either. He doesn't even work in a bakery. What was the counsellor going on about?

Mum said:

'I know you miss your dad, Pig. They are sending you on this holiday because they think you need a bit of help. Do you need a role model?'

I said:

'I eat rolls all the time. I had a ham roll

at lunch.'

Mum started to laugh again.

Then I said:

'What I would really like is for you and Dad

to come with me.'

Mum stopped laughing. She hugged me close.
Something wet dripped onto my head.

'Me too!' she said, 'Me too!

'But in the meanwhile – what about some
chips?'

The next **PIG** book is

PIG

and the

Long Fart

About the author

Barbara Catchpole was a teacher for thirty years and enjoyed every minute. She has three sons of her own who were always perfectly behaved and never gave her a second of worry.

Barbara also tells lies.